You Read to Me, I'll Read to You

Very Short Fairy Tales to Read Together

(in which wolves are tamed, trolls are transformed, and peas are triumphant)

by
MARY ANN HOBERMAN

Illustrated by
MICHAEL EMBERLEY

Megan Tingley Books

LITTLE, BROWN AND COMPANY

New York ❧ An AOL Time Warner Company

To the unknown authors of these tales, with love and gratitude
—M. A. H.

*To all the hardworking, unheralded comic artists—a constant source
of inspiration and humility*
—M. E.

Also to read together:

You Read to Me, I'll Read to You: Very Short Stories to Read Together

Text copyright © 2004 by Mary Ann Hoberman
Illustrations copyright © 2004 by Michael Emberley

First Edition

Library of Congress Cataloging-in-Publication Data

Hoberman, Mary Ann.
    You read to me, I'll read to you : very short fairy tales to read together / by Mary Ann
  Hoberman ; illustrated by Michael Emberley—1st ed.
      p. cm.
    "Megan Tingley books."
    ISBN 0-316-14611-0
    1. Readers (Primary) 2. Fairy tales. [1. Fairy tales.] I. Emberley, Michael, ill. II. Title.

PE1119.H63 2004
428.6—dc21   2003047445

10 9 8 7 6 5 4 3 2 1

TWP

Printed in Singapore

The illustrations for this book were done in gel pen, watercolor, and dry pastel on
90-lb. hot-press watercolor paper.
The text was set in Horley Old Style, and the display type is Shannon.

Table Of Contents

Author's Note:

Here is a sequel to the first *You Read to Me, I'll Read to You.* As in the preceding book, the short rhymed stories are like little plays for two voices that sometimes speak separately, sometimes in unison. However, the subject matter of these stories differs from the first book: Here, each one is a variation on a familiar fairy tale. But once again each story ends with a version of the same refrain:

> *You read to me!*
> *I'll read to you!*

As I said in the first book, I see the book's users as either a pair of beginning readers (two children, or a child and a parent who is in a literacy program) or one beginning and one more-advanced reader (either an older child or an adult). When you think about it, that includes just about every reader there is!

The stories in this book ring changes on eight traditional fairy tales. Therefore I recommend that parents and teachers make sure that their new readers are familiar with the original versions before going on to the stories in this book.

Once again I would like to acknowledge Literacy Volunteers of America. My work with them has provided me with the inspiration for these books, whose ongoing purpose is to encourage literacy by reading to, and listening to, each other.

Introduction

Here's another book,
Book two—

You read to me!

        I'll read to you!

We'll read each page
To one another—

You'll read one side,

        I the other.

But who will read—
Now guess this riddle—
When the words
Are in the middle?

The answer's easy!

        Plain as pie!

We'll read together,
You and I.

The Three Bears

I'm Goldilocks.

    I'm Baby Bear.

What pretty fur!

    What pretty hair!

Why are you here?

    You're in my bed.

I'm in your bed?

    That's what I said.
    Why are *you* here?

I lost my way.
I found your house
And thought I'd stay.

    And then you ate
    My porridge up
    And drank my milk
    Right from my cup.

Why, yes, I did.
You weren't there
And I was hungry,
Baby Bear.

    Well, now I'm very
    Hungry, too.

Oh, goodness me!
What shall we do?

    Where do you live?

Not very far.
A mile or two
From where we are.

I know the forest
Very well.
I'll take you home.
I'll trace your smell.

Why, Baby Bear,
You're very smart!

Get out of bed
And then we'll start.

When I get home,
Here's what I'll do:
I'll make some porridge
Just for you.

Will you add honey
For a treat?
(That's my favorite
Thing to eat.)

I'll add some honey
If you wish.
(You can even
Lick the dish.)

Yummy yum!
I love to lick!
What comes next?

I'll let you pick.

I pick a picture book
To share.

Why, that is perfect,
Baby Bear!

The Three Bears is
The one we'll do!
You'll read to me!
I'll read to you!

The Princess and the Pea

I'm the princess!

> I'm the pea!

Look at me!

> No, look at me!

Pea, you made me
Black and blue.

> I am flat
> Because of you.

I stayed up
The whole night long,
Wondering
Just what was wrong.

> I stayed up
> The whole night through,
> Squished and squashed
> Because of you.

I'm a princess,
Toe to chin.
Princesses
Have tender skin.

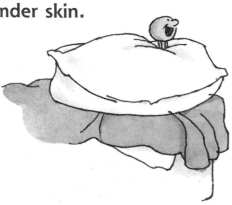

I'm the one
That proved you're real.
Think about
The way I feel.

You are just
A silly pea!
I'm a princess!
Look at me!

I'm not silly!
Not at all!
I can't help it
If I'm small.
Peas have feelings
Just like you.

Do they, Pea?

They do. It's true.

If it's true,
What can I do?

Put me in
Your wedding ring.
That would be
A special thing.

In my ring?
Oh, goodness me!
Not a diamond?

No, a pea.

Such a ring
I've never seen.
Still, you are
A pretty green.

Green and gold
Is really grand.
I'll look handsome
On your hand.

And every time
I look at you,
I'll think about
Our story, too.

Our story? Tell me
What you mean?

A story all about
A queen
Who made a princess
Just like me
Go to sleep
Upon a pea.

       And was the pea
       A pea like me?

Why, yes it was.
The very same.
*The Princess and
The Pea*'s its name.

       I'd like to read it.

I would, too.

    You read to me.
    I'll read to you.

11

Jack and the Beanstalk

My name is Jack,
The beanstalk lad.

> And I'm the ogre
> Jack made mad.

I lost our milk cow
In a trade.

> You got five beans.
> That's all you made.

My mother threw them out
That night
And in the morning
What a sight!
A beanstalk grew
That was so tall
We couldn't see
The top at all.

> You climbed it
> To the top and then
> You stole my magic
> Laying hen.

Your hen that lays
Gold eggs. Why, yes.
I stole your hen,
I do confess.

My bags of gold,
You stole them, too,
And then my golden harp.

That's true.

That was a naughty
Thing to do!

Now Mister Ogre,
Don't be mad.
I do admit
That I was bad,
But we were poor
And hungry, too.

You give them back
Or I'll eat *you!*

I'll give them back
If you agree
To sometimes lend
Your hen to me.

13

You're asking me
To lend my hen?

Not all the time.
Just now and then.
And also for
A special treat,
Please lend your harp.
It sounds so sweet.

Why, yes, it has
A lovely tone.
But don't forget,
It's just a loan!

A bag of gold
Perhaps you'd share?

A half-bag's all
That I can spare.

Now that's all settled
And we're friends
And that's the way
Our story ends.

Let's write it down.

Let's write it now.

We'll tell about
The beans and cow

And how the beanstalk
Grew and grew

And when our story
Is all through,
You'll read to me!
I'll read to you!

Little Red Riding Hood

Little Red Riding Hood's my name.
My grandma made my hood.
I'm visiting her house today.
She lives inside this wood.

My name is Big Bad Wolf, it is,
And I'm in Grandma's bed,
Pretending to be Grandma.
Her nightcap's on my head.

Why, Grandma dear, you're looking strange.
Your eyes are big and wide!

Oh, never mind, Red Riding Hood.
Just sit down by my side.

But Grandma dear, you look so odd.
Your teeth are very long!

Why, no, they're not, Red Riding Hood.
Believe me, nothing's wrong.

You're not my grandma! Not at all!
Just look me in the eye.

I am! I am! I really am!
I wouldn't tell a lie!

Oh, yes, you would! You mean old wolf,
I should have known it's you!

But see the nightcap on my head.
I'm Grandma through and through!

Now, Big Bad Wolf, tell me the truth.
What did you have to sup?

> Well, if you really have to know,
> I ate your grandma up.

You ate her up? You naughty wolf!

> I ate her in one bite.

Well, hurry, cough her up again!
I hope she's still all right.

> *Ahem! Ahaw! Kerchoo! Kerchaw!*

Oh, Grandma, you're not dead!
Now, Wolf, give Grandma back her cap
And give her back her bed.

> But I'm still starved, Red Riding Hood.
> What can I have to munch?

Well, if you promise to behave,
I'll take you out to lunch.

> We'll go out to a restaurant
> And while our dinners cook,
> We'll read a special story
> Out of a special book.

It's called *Little Red Riding Hood.*

> Just like your name, I see.

> Now let's begin. I'll read to you
> And then you'll read to me.

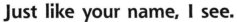

Cinderella

Cinderella
Is my name.

She's our sister.
What a shame!

All day long
I do my chores,
Washing clothes
And scrubbing floors.

All day long
We gobble sweets—
Candies, cakes,
And other treats.

I can't please them,
Though I try.

We are jealous.
That is why.

When the palace
Had a ball
And the King did
Ask us all,

We both played
A clever trick.
We pretended
She was sick.

When they left me,
Guess who came?
Fairy Godmother's
Her name!
My rags became
A gorgeous gown.
A carriage took me
Into town.

A beauty came
Into the ball.
The prince preferred her
To us all.

They didn't know
That it was I.
As midnight struck
I said good-by.
But as I hurried
Down the stair,
I lost one slipper
Of my pair.

Next day the prince
Sent out a crew
To find the owner
Of the shoe.

All day long
They looked for her
Until they came
To where we were.

We thought to get
Our feet to fit
We'd just chop off
A little bit.

Oh, don't do that!
Stepsisters, stop!
You'll hurt yourselves!
You mustn't chop!
It's not your fault
You wear size nine.
The only foot it fits
Is mine.

It's just not fair!
It's just not right!
You should have stayed
At home last night.

Now don't be selfish.
Don't be mean.
You're talking to
The future queen.

You'll be the queen?
Why, that is true!
All right, we'll both
Be nice to you.

Well, if you're nice
As nice can be,
I'll let you both
Come live with me.

In the palace?
Oh, what fun!
All our naughty
Days are done!

But we can read
The old tale, too—
Cinderella—
Read it through.
You read to me.
I'll read to you.

The Three Little Pigs

I'm Big Bad Wolf.

        I'm Little Pig.

You're very small.

        You're very big.
        But now I've got you
        In my pot.

The water's getting
Very hot.

        I'll cook you up
        And make a stew.

Why, that's an awful
Thing to do.

        Now that's a silly
        Thing to say.
        You ate my brother
        Yesterday.

Why, so I did!
I had forgot.
(This water's getting
Really hot.)

And on the day before
It's you
Who ate my other
Brother, too.

Did I do that?
That wasn't nice.
(Could you put in
A little ice?)

They built their houses
In the town.
You huffed and puffed
And blew them down.

Well, they were made
Of straw and sticks
While yours is made
Of good strong bricks.

First I built
My house of bricks,
And then I fooled you
With my tricks.

And now you've got me
In your pot.
This water's really
Really hot!

Say you're sorry
Loud and clear.

I'm sorry. Let me
Out of here!

Louder! Clearer!
Give a shout!

I'M SORRY, PIG!
NOW LET ME OUT!

Now do you promise
To be nice?

I promise, Pig.

Then here's some ice.
Sit down and cool
Yourself a bit.
I'll read you something
While you sit.

What will you read?

> A tale that's true.
> A tale about
> Both me and you.

Can I read, too?

> If you know how.

Of course I do.

> Then let's start now.

We'll read *Three Little Pigs*
Right through.
You'll read to me.
I'll read to you.

The Little Red Hen and the Grain of Wheat

I'm Little Red Hen.
I planted the wheat.
I dug up the soil
In the dust and the heat.

And I am the Duck
And I have to admit
That I did not help her,
Not one little bit.

I'm Little Red Hen.
With my rake and my hoe
I weeded my garden
And helped it to grow.

And I am the Cat
And all through the spring
I did nothing either,
Not one little thing.

I'm Little Red Hen.
I watered my grain
All summer long
And I did not complain.

And I am the Dog.
I stayed in my bed
And pulled all my covers
Right over my head.

I worked in my garden
Until it was fall
And the small grain of wheat
Had grown ripe and quite tall.

We watched as she worked
While the harvest time passed
And she threshed it and ground it
And baked it at last.

And then when the bread
Was baked golden and nice,
I went and I asked you
If you'd like a slice.

And all of us answered,
As you may well guess,
With a shout and a cheer
And a great big loud YES!

But you didn't help me.
I worked all alone
And cared for my garden
Until it was grown.

And all of us answered,
We're sorry indeed!
We'll help you the next time
When you plant a seed.

Is that a true promise?
Do all of you swear
To help me the next time
And do your fair share?

And all of us answered,
Why, Little Red Hen,
We'll never be lazy
And selfish again!

Well, if you are sure
That you'll do as you say,
Then here are your slices.

Oh, hip, hip, hooray!
This bread is delicious,
So golden and brown,
And now that we've eaten,
We think we'll sit down.

I think I'll sit with you
And take a short rest.
I'll read you a story,
The one I like best.

What story is that, Hen?

A story I know.
We'll read it together.
We'll go nice and slow.

And what is it called, Hen?

Why, something quite sweet.
The Little Red Hen and
The Small Grain of Wheat.

Why, that sounds like you, Hen.

You're all in it, too.

You'll read it to me and
I'll read it to you.

The Three Billy Goats Gruff

I am the biggest billy goat.

> I am a great big troll.
> I'm standing guard upon my bridge.

I'm going for a stroll.

> But I won't let you cross my bridge.
> Unless you pay a toll.

Why, I'm the biggest billy goat!
You can't do that to me!

> But I'm an old ferocious troll
> As you can plainly see.

Do you charge lots of money, Troll?

> I only charge a cent.

What do you use your money for?

> I have to pay my rent.

I pay bills for my brothers, Troll.
They both depend on me.

> And I support my two young trolls.
> I, too, must work for three.

You poor old troll, if I had known
Your worries and your woes,
I never would have bothered you
Or scared you, goodness knows!

And Billy Goat, if *I* had known
Your troubles and your cares
I never would have frightened *you*
Or given *you* such scares.

Why, thank you, Troll.
That's very nice.

I'd like to thank you, too.

And now that we've become good friends,
What would you like to do?

Why, I would like to dip my toes
Into the mountain brook.

And I would like to poke my nose
Into a storybook
About three billy goats named Gruff
Who took a mountain stroll
And went across a mountain bridge
And fooled a great big troll.

You fool me in that story?

Why, yes, I fear we do.

Well, never mind, you read to me
And I will read to you.

The End

And so our fairy tales
Are through.

We've read them all.
What shall we do?

We could reread them.

Yes, we could.

That might be fun.

That might be good.

But then, again,
We could read some
Of those old tales
That these are from.

And I know something else
As well.
There are more fairy tales
To tell.

Other ones
We haven't read?
Other ones
To read instead?

Many more
That we can add.
Funny, scary,
Happy, sad,
Short ones, long ones,
Old and new.

Well, why not start
To read a few?
You read to me.
I'll read to you.